To Harry

Text and illustrations ©

First published in Gre
Frances Lincoln Limit
Torriano Avenue, Lon

British Library Cataloguing in Publication Data
French, Fiona, *1944—*
  Anancy and Mr Dry-Bone
  I. Title
  823.914

ISBN 0-7112-0672-4 hardback
ISBN 0-7112-0787-9 paperback
Printed in Hong Kong

9 8 7 6 5

ANANCY
AND
MR DRY-BONE

FIONA FRENCH

FRANCES LINCOLN

Mr Dry-Bone lived in a big house
on top of a hill.
He was very rich and he wanted
to marry Miss Louise.

Anancy lived in a small house
at the foot of the hill.
He was very poor and he wanted to
marry Miss Louise as well.

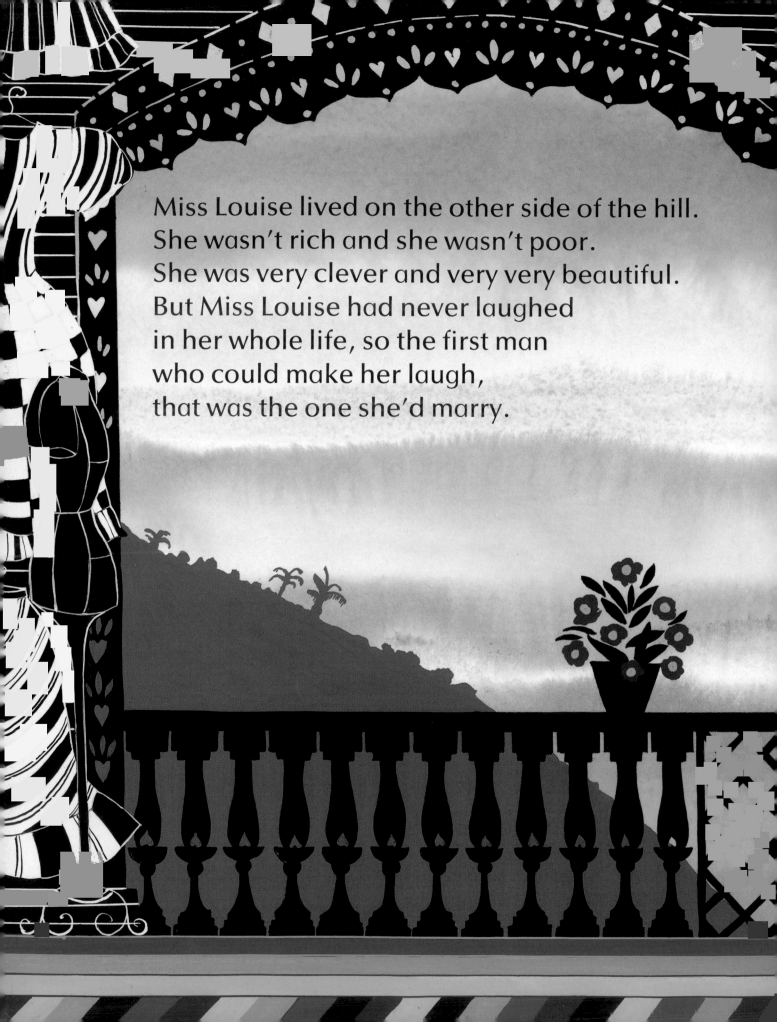

Miss Louise lived on the other side of the hill.
She wasn't rich and she wasn't poor.
She was very clever and very very beautiful.
But Miss Louise had never laughed
in her whole life, so the first man
who could make her laugh,
that was the one she'd marry.

Mr Dry-Bone knocked on Miss Louise's door. He was all dressed up in his very best clothes.
"Good evening," he said.
"I've brought all my powerful conjuring tricks and I'm going to make you laugh."
"Well," said Miss Louise, "this I've got to see."

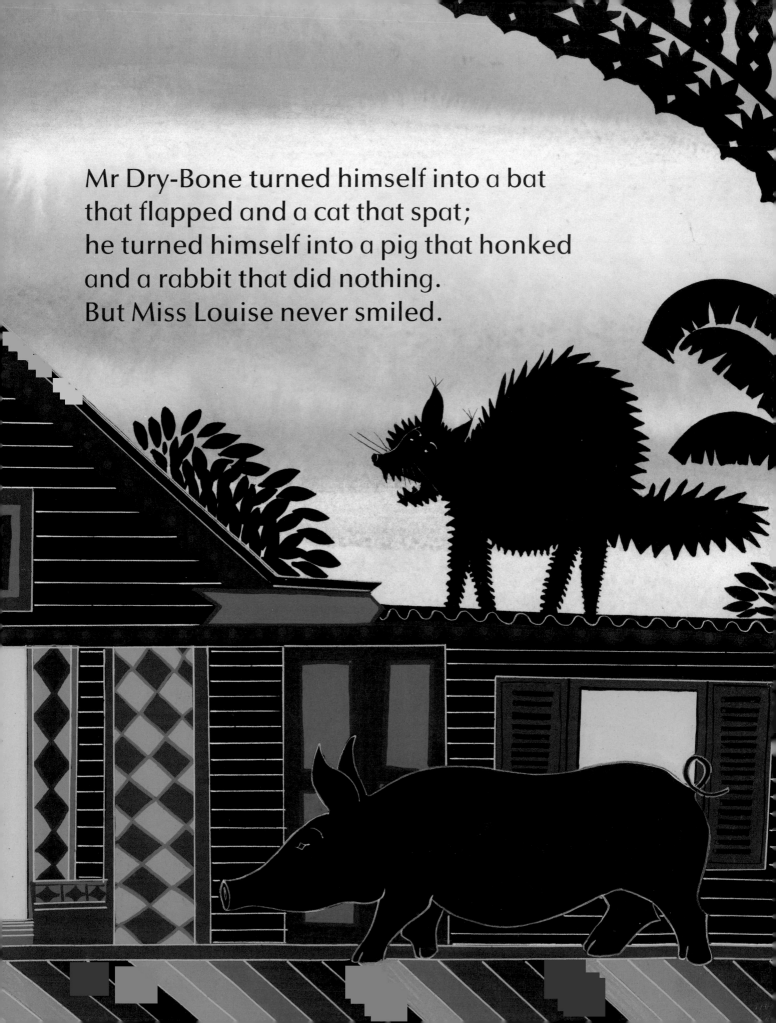

Mr Dry-Bone turned himself into a bat
that flapped and a cat that spat;
he turned himself into a pig that honked
and a rabbit that did nothing.
But Miss Louise never smiled.

Mr Dry-Bone turned somersaults and cartwheels and stood upsidedown on the ceiling.
But still Miss Louise never smiled.
Anancy said to himself,
"I can do better than that."

Anancy went to Tiger and said,
"Lend me your best evening suit,
I'm going to visit Miss Louise."
Tiger said, "My evening suit
is at the cleaners right now,
but you can borrow my jogging suit."

Anancy went to see Dog.
"Lend me your top hat,
I'm going to visit Miss Louise."
Dog said, "My top hat got
crushed the other day but
you can borrow my
hunting hat."

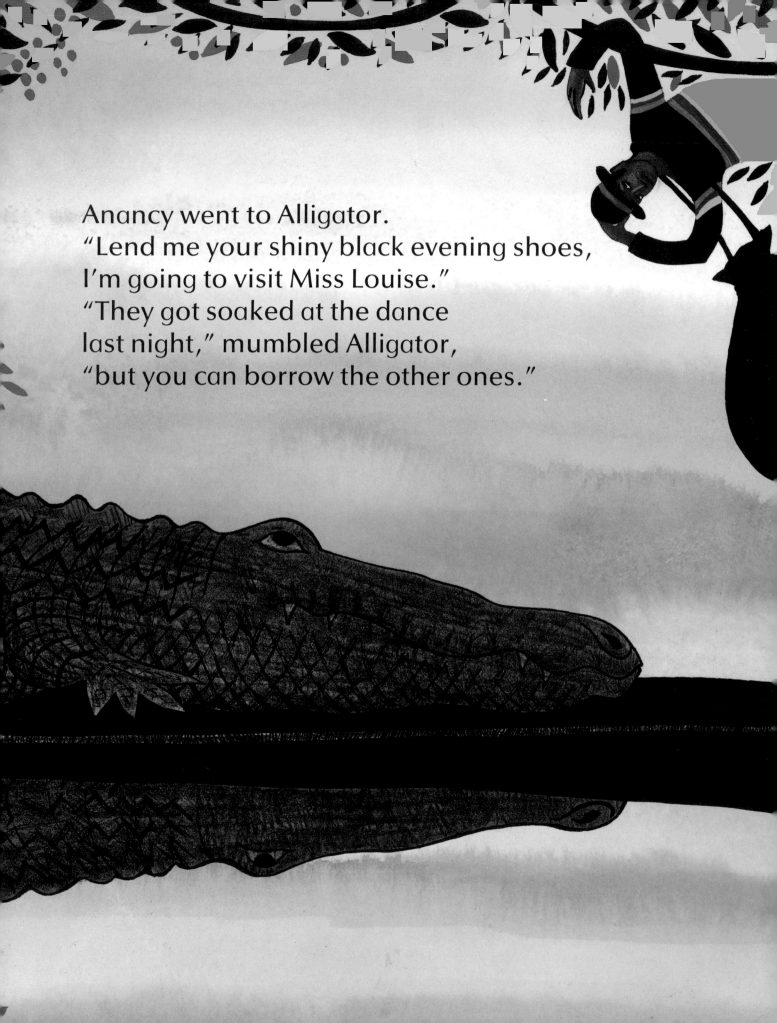

Anancy went to Alligator.
"Lend me your shiny black evening shoes,
I'm going to visit Miss Louise."
"They got soaked at the dance
last night," mumbled Alligator,
"but you can borrow the other ones."

Monkey swung through the trees
and called to Anancy,
"You'll need a tie when you
visit Miss Louise."

Parrot squawked and dropped
some feathers.
"Put these in your hunting hat, Anancy,
they'll look real good when you
visit Miss Louise."

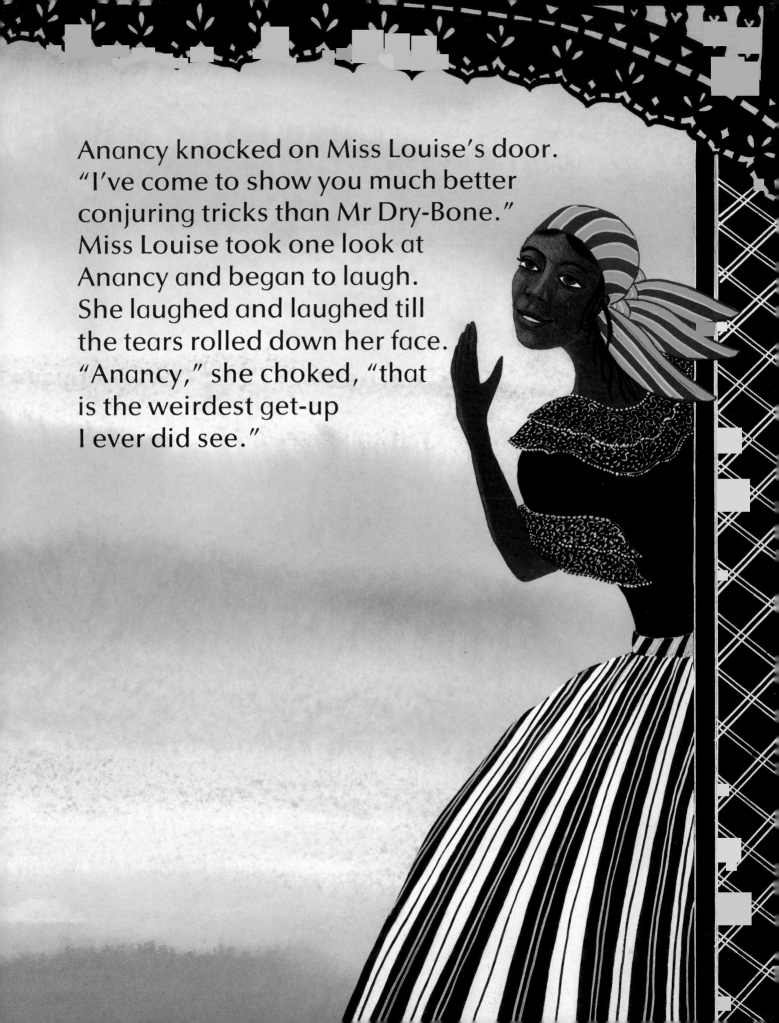

Anancy knocked on Miss Louise's door.
"I've come to show you much better
conjuring tricks than Mr Dry-Bone."
Miss Louise took one look at
Anancy and began to laugh.
She laughed and laughed till
the tears rolled down her face.
"Anancy," she choked, "that
is the weirdest get-up
I ever did see."

Everyone laughed.
Even Mr Dry-Bone.
"OK, you win," he said.

So Anancy married Miss Louise,
and they all lived happily
ever after.